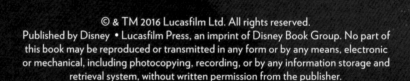

For information address Disney • Lucasfilm Press,
1101 Flower Street, Glendale, California 91201.

Printed in China
First Hardcover Edition, July 2016   10 9 8 7 6 5 4 3 2

ISBN 978-1-4847-8668-0
FAC-023680-17198

Visit the official *Star Wars* website at: www.starwars.com
This book was printed on paper created from a sustainable source.

STAR WARS

Leia and the Ewoks

Disney • LUCASFILM PRESS

Los Angeles • New York

Book Ten

L
uke Skywalker looked around the forest moon of Endor. He had landed there with Princess Leia, Han Solo, Chewbacca, R2-D2, and C-3PO. The rebels were on a mission. They were looking for a secret bunker that hid a special machine—a machine that could help them destroy the Death Star!

As the rebels snuck through the forest, they spotted two stormtroopers on speeder bikes.

"Should we try and go around?" Princess Leia asked.

"It'll take time," Luke replied.

But Han had an idea. "Chewie and I will take care of this," he said. "You stay here."

Luke warned Han to be quiet, but Han had other ideas. He and Chewie snuck up on the stormtroopers and attacked! One scout turned and punched Han. "Go for help! Go!" he shouted to the second scout. Chewbacca used his bowcaster to shoot down the escaping scout's speeder bike. But two other scouts hopped on their bikes and took off into the forest!

Luke and Leia climbed aboard the first scouts' bikes and sped after the others. They couldn't let the stormtroopers warn the Empire of their presence on Endor.

"Keep on that one. I'll take these two," Luke called. And with that, he veered off, leaving Leia behind.

With his deft maneuvering and quick thinking, Luke swung behind the enemies. Taking aim, Luke fired. One of the speeders crashed into a nearby tree and exploded. But Luke tumbled off his speeder. Using his lightsaber, he swiped at the second speeder, which crashed.

Meanwhile, Leia was side by side with her target. But she wasn't prepared when he pulled his blaster and fired on her. A shot hit her speeder bike engine, throwing her off. Her speeder bike crashed. The biker scout looked back victoriously. *Boom!* He crashed, too. Relieved, Leia lost consciousness.

When Leia awoke, she was alone in the forest, with no way to get back to her friends. Suddenly, a short, fuzzy creature came up to her. It was an Ewok named Wicket. He had never seen a human before, and he didn't like the look of Leia. He poked her gently with his spear.

"Cut it out," Leia said, standing up and brushing herself off.

Leia sighed and walked over to a fallen tree. "Looks like I'm stuck here," she said. "Trouble is, I don't know where *here* is!"

Leia looked at the Ewok again. "Maybe you can help me," she said, offering the Ewok some food.

The little Ewok perked up.

Suddenly, a blaster shot fired their way! Wicket rolled under the log, out of sight, just before a stormtrooper came up behind Leia. Wicket didn't want the stormtrooper to hurt his new friend. He smacked the trooper on the leg with his spear!

Taking advantage of the distraction, Leia knocked the stormtrooper out. She wanted to go back to her friends, but the Ewok had other plans. *"Yub, yub,"* he said, leading her down a long winding path deep into the forest.

Meanwhile, Luke had reunited with his friends. When they realized that Leia hadn't returned, Luke, Han, Chewbacca, and the droids set out to look for her. They were worried.

Suddenly, Chewie growled. He smelled a piece of meat—and he was hungry! He ran over to the meat, which was hanging from a tall stick.

"Chewie, wait, wait, don't!" Luke cried.

But the warning came too late. When Chewie tried to take the meat, a net rose around the friends and captured them. It was a trap!

R2-D2 used a mechanical blade to cut them out of the giant net. Luckily, the trap hadn't been set by stormtroopers. It had been set by Ewoks. The fuzzy little creatures surrounded Luke and the others, pointing their spears at the rebels.

"Hey, point that thing somewhere else!" Han said gruffly, grabbing the nearest spear. That made the Ewoks mad. They growled and moved closer.

Suddenly, the Ewoks spotted C-3PO. The droid's golden metal body glinted in the sunlight. The Ewoks gasped! They began chanting and bowing toward him.

"I do believe they think I am some sort of god," C-3PO said.

Han was not happy to hear that. But Luke persuaded him and the others to go along with the Ewoks to their village. They didn't want to hurt the creatures, so they'd need to figure out a way to escape without fighting.

When the friends arrived at the village, Leia was there.

"Leia!" Luke and Han exclaimed together.

"These are my friends," Leia told the Ewoks. "Threepio, tell them they must be set free."

But the Ewoks wouldn't listen to C-3PO. They tied up Luke, Han, and Chewie and began stacking firewood under them.

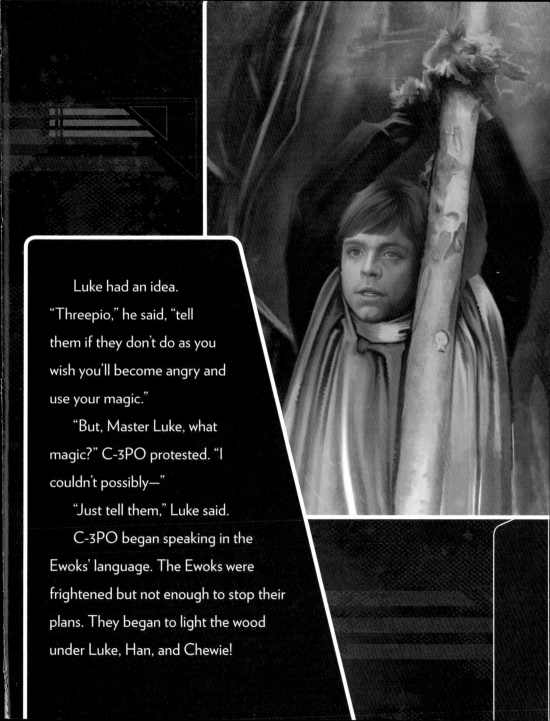

Luke had an idea. "Threepio," he said, "tell them if they don't do as you wish you'll become angry and use your magic."

"But, Master Luke, what magic?" C-3PO protested. "I couldn't possibly—"

"Just tell them," Luke said.

C-3PO began speaking in the Ewoks' language. The Ewoks were frightened but not enough to stop their plans. They began to light the wood under Luke, Han, and Chewie!

Just when Han was sure that they were goners, Luke closed his eyes. He used the Force to raise the chair C-3PO was sitting on into the air!

"Ahhh! What's happening?" C-3PO cried. "Master Luke, help!"

But Luke continued to use the Force. C-3PO hovered high above the Ewok tribe, terrifying the furry creatures.

Quickly, the Ewok leader ordered the others to set Luke, Han, and Chewie free. The tribe members obeyed and cut the friends loose.

Luke smiled and used the Force to lower C-3PO back to the ground.

Later that night, everyone listened as C-3PO told the Ewok tribe the story of the rebels' adventures fighting the Empire. Leia and her friends couldn't understand the Ewok language C-3PO was using, but they enjoyed listening anyway.

Suddenly, the Ewoks started chattering anxiously among themselves.

"What's going on?" Han asked Leia.

Leia shrugged. "I don't know."

The Ewoks banged their ceremonial drums and started to sing.

"Wonderful!" C-3PO exclaimed. "We are now part of the tribe."

The Ewoks ran up to hug Han and Leia. Wicket was especially fond of hugging Han.

"Just what I always wanted!" Han said with a half grin, gently pushing the fuzzy creature away.

Now the Ewoks would help the rebels in their fight against the Empire. Both the rebels and the stormtroopers had learned that although the Ewoks were small and cute, they would defend themselves when threatened.

The forest moon of Endor was their home, and the Ewoks would fight fiercely to keep the Empire from destroying it. The rebels were glad to have the furry warriors on their side.